W9-CMP-236

Slugs in Love

by
Susan Pearson

illustrated by
Kevin O'Malley

Herbie   Marylou

Amazon Children's Publishing

Text copyright © 2012 by Susan Pearson
Illustrations copyright © 2012 by Kevin O'Malley
First Amazon Children's Publishing paperback edition, 2012

All rights reserved

Amazon Publishing
Attn: Amazon Children's Publishing
P.O. Box 400818
Las Vegas, NV 89149
www.amazon.com/amazonchildrenspublishing

Library of Congress Cataloging-in-Publication Data
Pearson, Susan.
Slugs in love / by Susan Pearson ; illustrated by Kevin O'Malley.— 1st ed.
p. cm.
Summary: Marylou and Herbie, two garden slugs, write love poems in slime
to one another but have trouble actually meeting.
978-0-7614-5311-6 (hardcover) 978-0-7614-6248-4 (paperback)
[1. Slugs (Mollusks)—Fiction. 2. Poetry—Fiction. 3. Love—Fiction.]
I. O'Malley, Kevin, 1961- ill. II. Title.
PZ8.3.P27473Slu 2006
[E]—dc22
2005027073

Book design by Symon Chow

Printed in Malaysia (T)

10 9 8 7 6 5 4 3 2 1

For Rosemary and Dave
_S.P.

Marylou loved everything about Herbie—how his slime trail glistened in the dark, how he could stretch himself thin to squeeze inside the cellar window, how he always found the juiciest tomato. Though she never spoke a single word to him—she was too shy—she thought about Herbie every morning and every night and most of the hours in between.

On Monday, while she grazed in the strawberry patch, Herbie filled her mind and a love poem filled her heart. She wrote it in slime on the watering can.

Strawberries are red.
Blueberries are blue.
Herbie is handsome.
Love,
Marylou

The next morning, Herbie found it. He looked around. There were already at least sixty slugs in the garden. Which one, he wondered, was Marylou?

Herbie decided to send a message back. He wrote it on the garden hoe.

Marylou, which one are you?
Meet me here at half past two.
Yours truly,
      Herbie

But the gardener put the hoe
away in the barn, so Marylou never
saw Herbie's message.

On Tuesday, while Marylou was hiding from the sun in the ivy, she saw Herbie hiding under a stone, and a poem came immediately to mind. She wrote it on the wheelbarrow later that day.

"Marylou loves Herrrrrrbie!" teased Jethro on Wednesday morning.

Herbie blushed. "Who *is* Marylou?" he asked, but Jethro didn't know either.

Herbie sent another message. This time he wrote it on a fence where it would stay put.

To Marylou:
You could make my life complete!
I'd love to meet someone so sweet,
Tell me where and I'll be there,
Sincerely,
Herbie

But that afternoon it rained and his letter washed away.

Even when Marylou was sleeping, poems to Herbie filled her dreams. She woke early and wrote another poem on the scarecrow.

"That Marylou is some poet!" said Sammy.

"Do you know her?" Herbie asked excitedly.

"I think she's the brownish one," said Sammy.

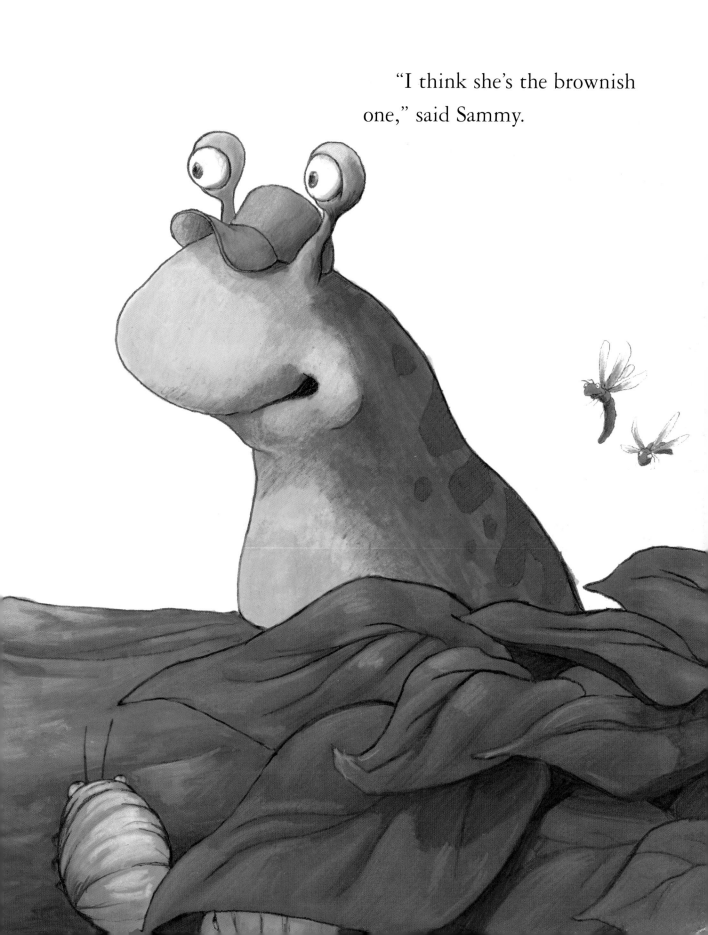

All day long Herbie searched for a brownish slug, but next to the brown dirt, they all looked a little brown. Herbie left another message on the watermelons.

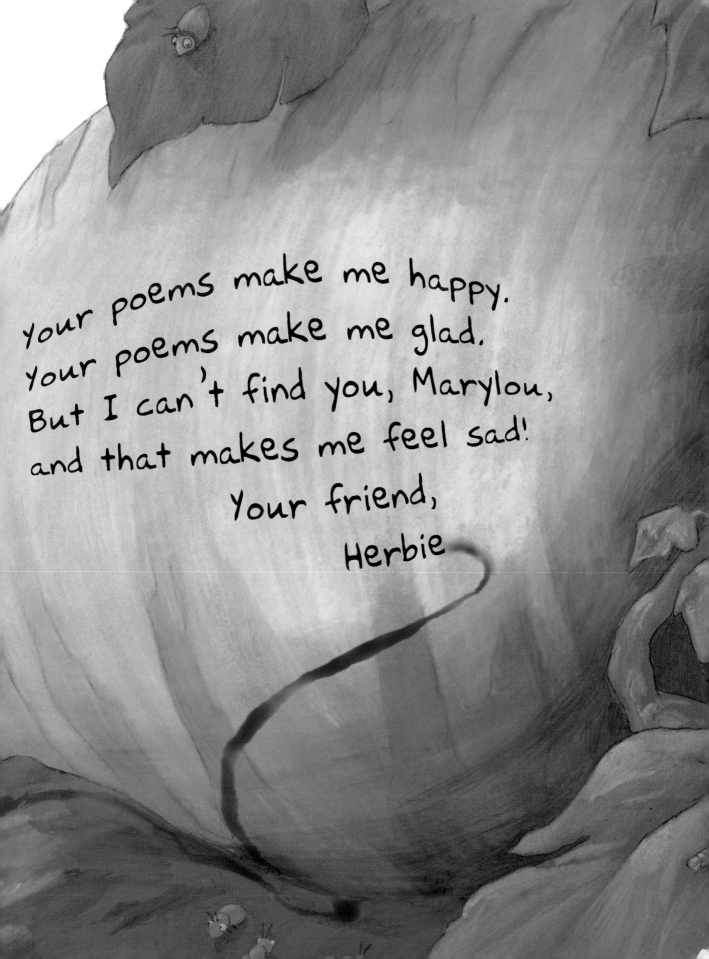

Your poems make me happy.
Your poems make me glad.
But I can't find you, Marylou,
and that makes me feel sad!
Your friend,
Herbie

But Marylou was in the squash patch that day and didn't see Herbie's note. She left another poem behind on the zucchini.

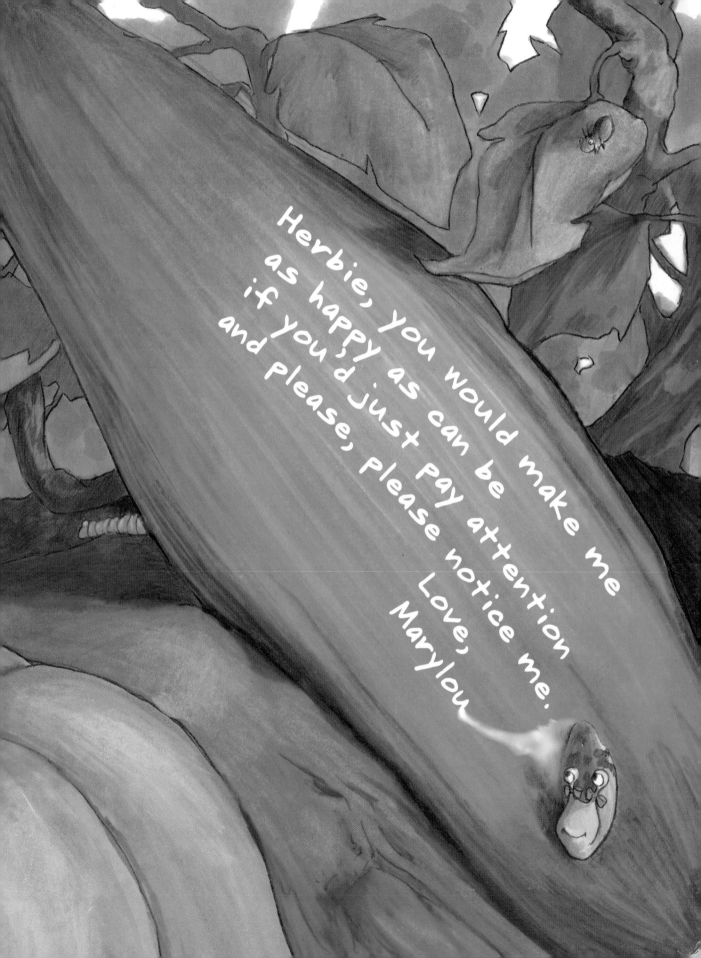

Herbie was at his wit's end. He *had* been noticing her! Well, her poems anyway. And he'd asked everyone he could think of if they knew her.

"I think she's the greenish one," said Homer.

"I think she's the pinkish one," said Jodelle.

"Maybe she's the one who likes tomatoes," said Adelaide.

"*All* slugs like tomatoes!" said Herbie.

But Adelaide had given him an idea.

Herbie climbed to the top of the tallest tomato plant. On his way back down, he wrote a message.

And that night, when Marylou went out to snack on a tomato, she found Herbie's message glistening in the garden! What joy! What gladness! What delight! Marylou could hardly contain herself as she hurried to the barn.

The next morning, the first thing Herbie saw was:

As always, when she saw Herbie, poetry filled
Marylou's head. She said:
 "Herbie, I am Marylou.
 We meet at last. How do you do?"
 Herbie was tongue-tied. Suddenly he felt shy.
But at last he blurted out:
 "I am fine.
 Will you be mine?"

Marylou and Herbie
lived happily ever after.